POKA AND PEANUT

PLAYTIME POEMS

WRITTEN BY ALEXANDRIA COX
ILLUSTRATED BY ROBERT SEGURA

WHO ARE YOU?

When I get all grown up,
you'll be proud!

Just support me
and help me out!

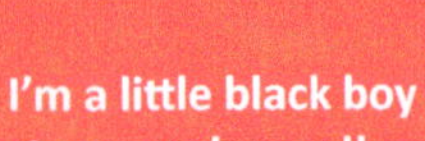

I'm a little black boy
strong and proud!

Here is my homeland,
here is my crown.

I'm a little black girl
strong and proud!

Here is my homeland,
here is my crown.

When I get all grown up,
you'll be proud!

Just support me
and help me out!

LOOK AT ME
Mama, mama
look at me!
I'm something for the world to see!
My friends may doubt me... but I believe,
I can be whatever I want to be!

Daddy, daddy
look at me!
I'm something for the
world to see!

My friends may doubt me... but I believe,
I can be whatever I want to be!

MIRROR

When I look in the mirror,
do you know what I see?
I see a young black king
looking back at me!

Although, times get tough...
I know one thing!
The only thing better than me,
is a better me.

When I look in the mirror,
do you know what I see?
I see a young black Queen
looking back at me!

Although, times get tough...
I know one thing!
The only thing better than me,
 is a better me.

RESPONSIBILITIES

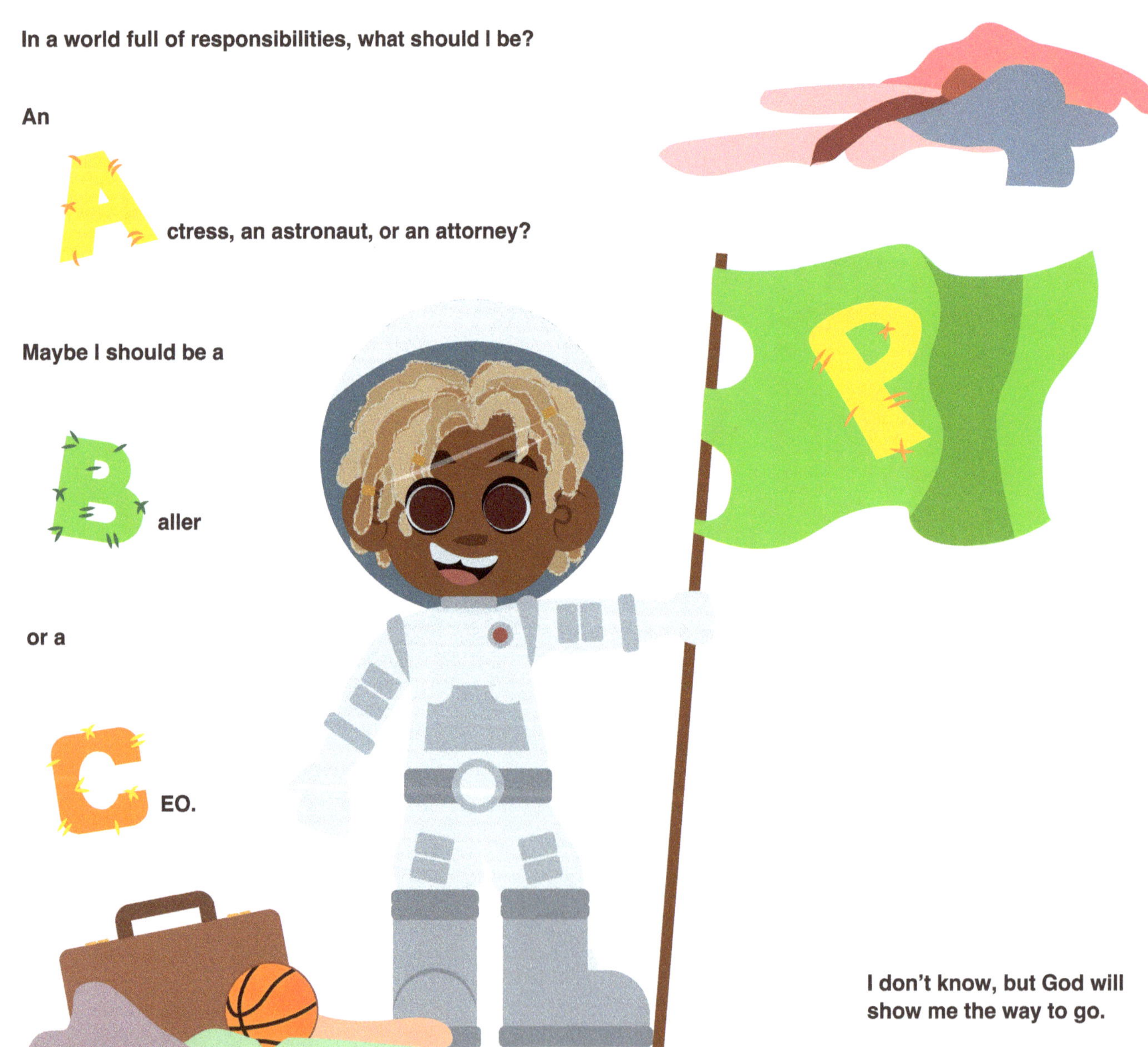

In a world full of responsibilities, what should I be?

An **A**ctress, an astronaut, or an attorney?

Maybe I should be a **B**aller

or a **C**EO.

I don't know, but God will show me the way to go.

In a world full of responsibilities what should I be?

A

Dentist, a developer, or a dancer?

or maybe an

Economist or an EMT.

I'm not sure but God will show me what's for me.
In a world full of responsibilities, I just want to be... A wonderful addition to society.

P-E-T-T-Y

If they be mean to you,
don't be mean back.
That's P-E-T-T-Y!

Don't be petty
just say bye-bye.

You can't be number one
if you keep acting like number two.
Lead by example,
show them how bosses move!

Hopefully one day
they'll be a boss like you!

LIFE

Life goes up and life goes down.
Twist, bumps, and turn-arounds.
It's kind of like flying a kite.
You have to do a little running
before things catch flight.

Life goes up and life goes down.
Twist, bumps, and turn-arounds.
It's kind of like drawing a crown.
Your pencil goes many different ways,
but somehow it ends up round.

BIG HEART

There once was a girl with such a **BIG HEART**, she didn't know what to do. She would help everyone, including me and you. Until one day she needed help and didn't know what to do.

Her grandpa explained that helping people is okay, but you have to make sure that you have someone there when it's time for you.

There once was a
boy with such a
BIG HEART,
he didn't know
what to do.

He would help
everyone, including
me and you. Until
one day he needed
help and didn't
know what to do.

His grandma explained
that helping people is
okay but you have to
make sure that you have
someone there when it's
time for you.

It's one thing that their
grandparents did not know
that they knew…

Helping others only makes
God want to help you.

BUSINESS

I'm a **CEO**,
you have an **LLC**
and they have a **501C3**.
The world has roles that have to be played.
The best thing about it is…

WE ALL GET PAID!

Business is business but we must see…
that the business world has
NO LIMIT economically.

CHOICES

Our lives are the products of our choices.
What will you pick?

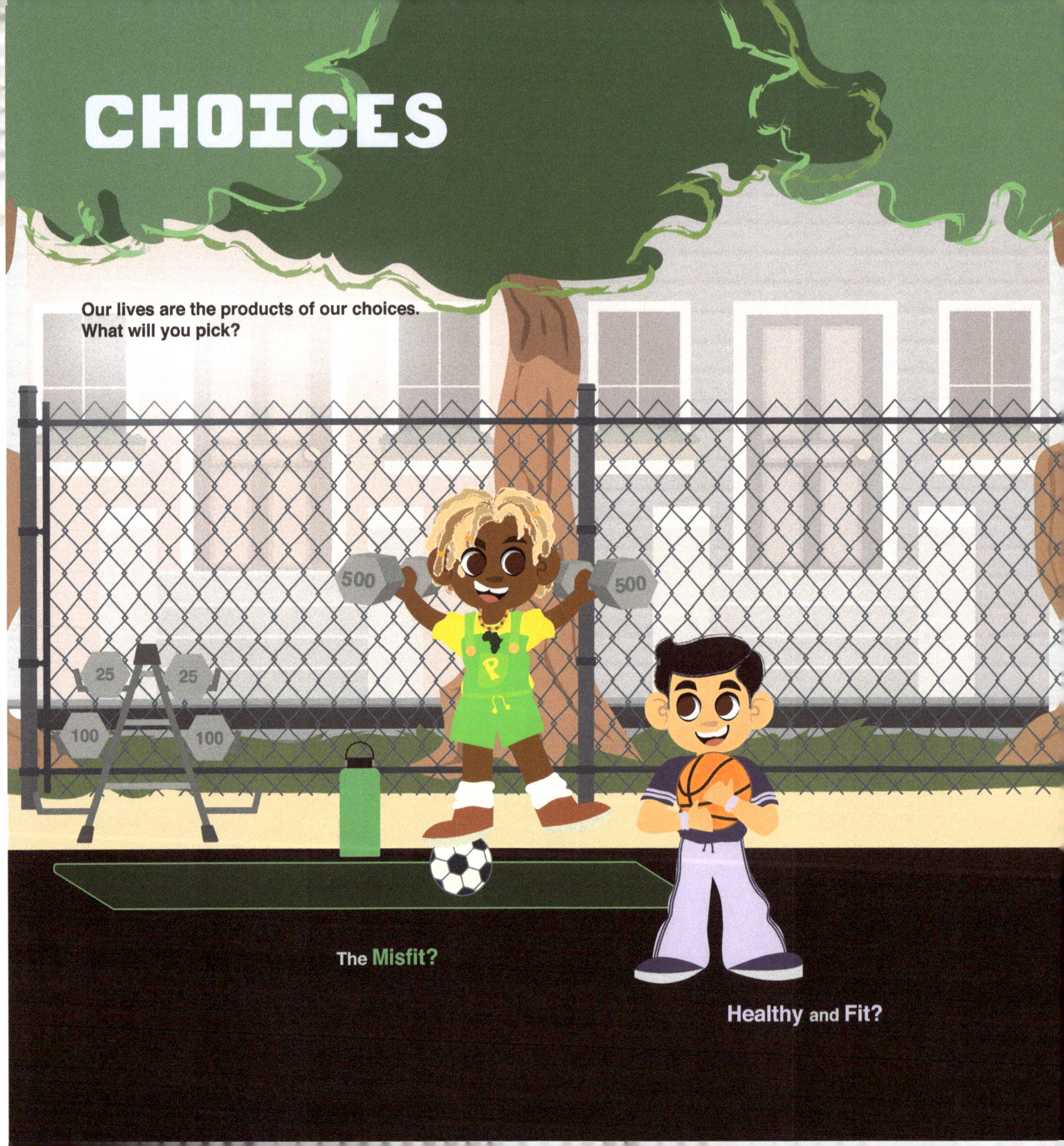

Or Beautiful and Thick?
You may not know now
but whatever you pick,
remember it's your life
and it's about what you see fit.

FAMILY
Oh Daddy, I want to be like you.
BIG AND STRONG,
and know what to do!
Paid!
Oh mama, I want to be like you.
It's like you got 8 ARMS
you are always doing the do!

Oh Granny, I want to be like you.

You COOK WITHOUT MEASURING,
it's like the food tells you!

Oh Pawpaw, I want to be just like you.

You are ALWAYS TALKING,
but your lips never move!

Oh baby, we want to be just like you.

A WALKING SPONGE,
you know what everybody do!

FLOUR

YOU ARE WHAT YOU EAT!
Daddy said...
"You are what you eat"
so I pick beans
to replace my meat.
Mama said...
"You are what you eat"
so I pick healthy things like
baby bananas
as my sweet.

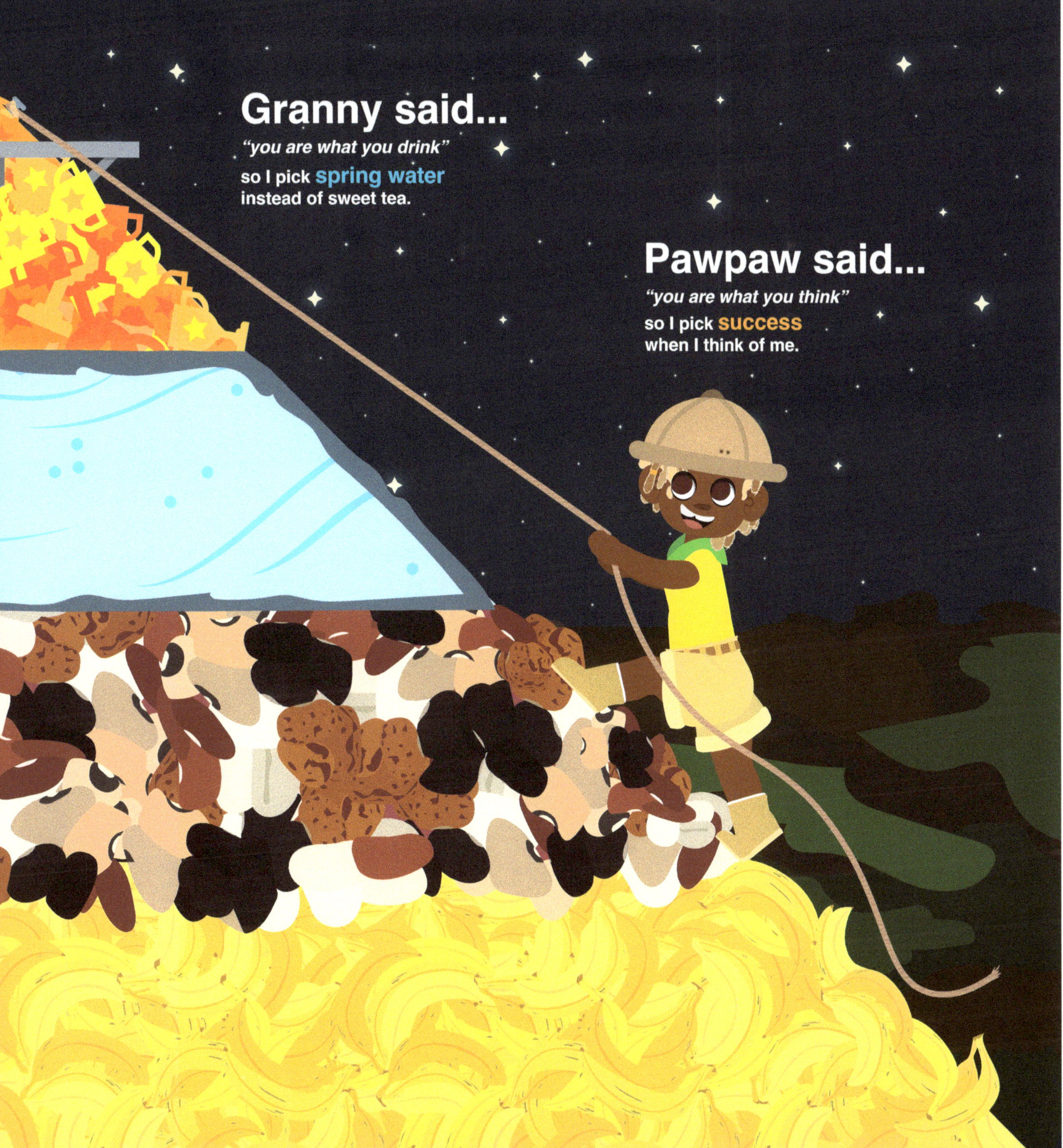

Granny said...
"you are what you drink"
so I pick spring water
instead of sweet tea.

Pawpaw said...
"you are what you think"
so I pick success
when I think of me.

LA-LA-LU

Memaw's famous La-La-Lu.
Also known as survival stew.
Vegetables, Beans, Pasta, and Rice,
all drenched in tomato sauce and served real nice.
We never knew the ingredients,
we just knew that she did the do.
A bowl full of wonders and love
La-La-Lu.
Memaw's Survival Stew,
if the dogs don't like it,
I do!

TEXAS
I live in Texas!
where it's cold and rainy one day,
then it's hot and sunny the next!

And if you wait five minutes
you just might see
some sleet
or snow,
but *youuuu* should know
that sleet and snow
don't stick!
But living in Texas
WILL MAKE YOU SICK!!!

THINGS TO REMEMBER

I SHOULD listen more than I speak.

I SHOULD walk the way that I talk.

I SHOULD stand for what I believe.

I SHOULD have faith in what I want to achieve.

I SHOULD be what the world needs.

I SHOULD BE A BETTER ME.

CLEAN

Wash your hands,
   brush your teeth,

clean your face,
and take a bath

To dry off,
we stomp our feet
and to stay clean,

WE REPEAT!

Introducción

A la hora de confeccionar, arreglar o "salvar" una prenda el dominio de la labor de la costura es esencial. Porque coser no es solo enhebrar una aguja y dar puntadas. Existen distintos tipos de costuras que se emplean para esas diferentes situaciones.

Si bien las máquinas más modernas y evolucionadas realizan casi todas las técnicas, conocerlas es imprescindible para aquellas mujeres que recién comienzan y que desean adquirir experiencia y prolijidad en la costura.

Esta entrega nos enseñará las nociones básicas de la costura y confección para coser a mano, hacer dobladillos, pinzas y colocar cierres; tomar medidas correctamente para aprovechar las telas al máximo o usar una máquina de coser.

Índice

Escuela de costura / Angelita. - 1a ed . - Ciudad Autónoma de Buenos Aires : Dos Editores, 2016.
24 p. ; 20 x 20 cm.

1. Manualidades. I. Título.
CDD 745.5

© Dos Tintas SA
Balcarce 711 Ciudad Autónoma de Buenos Aires Argentina
info@doseditores.com

Hecho el depósito que marca la Ley 11.723
Queda prohibida la reproducción total o parcial de esta obra por cualquier medio o procedimiento, sin el permiso por escrito de la editorial.

Impreso en Argentina
COLORGRAF
Caviglia 27, Wilde, Pcia. de Buenos Aires.
Agosto 2016

Las herramientas de la costura

Para realizar tareas de costura y adquirir experiencia en la confección y arreglos de indumentaria se necesita habilidad, mucha práctica y un equipo de herramientas básicas. Entre ellas no podemos dejar de mencionar las siguientes:

Alfileres

De acero, finos y con puntas filosas. Por prevención, se deben descartar los que estén dañados u oxidados pues pueden dejar marcas en las ropas y telas.

Agujas

(para coser a mano y a máquina)

Hay agujas de diversos tipos: para coser a mano o máquina, para telas finas o gruesas, cortas o largas, finas o gruesas. Cada trabajo demandará una distinta y eso solo lo descubriremos con la práctica. Lo básico es que las agujas sean de buena calidad, limpias, sin óxido y con la punta perfectamente afilada.

Dedal

Es importante adquirir la costumbre de utilizar el dedal. Cumple varias funciones: protege el dedo, da rapidez a la costura y sirve para alisar la misma mientras se trabaja.